America's Leaders

THE
Attorney
GENERAL

by Joanne Mattern

BLACKBIRCH®
PRESS

THOMSON

GALE

San Diego • Detroit • New York • San Francisco • Cleveland • New Haven, Conn. • Waterville, Maine • London • Munich

AR= MG (7.5) 1.0

THOMSON

GALE

LIBRARY OF CONGRESS CATALOGING-IN-PUBLICATION DATA

Mattern, Joanne, 1963-
  Attorney general / by Joanne Mattern.
    p. cm. — (America's leaders)
  Includes index.
  Summary: Discusses the duties of the Attorney General, how one gets this job, where one works, the daily routine, and other facts about the position.
  ISBN 1-56711-278-1 (lib. : alk. paper)
  1. United States. Dept. of Justice. Office of the Attorney General—Juvenile literature.
2. Attorneys general—United States—Juvenile literature. 3. Justice, Administration of—United States—Juvenile literature. [1. United States. Dept. of Justice. Office of the Attorney General. 2. Attorneys general. 3. Cabinet officers.] I. Title. II. Series. America's leaders series.

KF5107.Z9 M38 2003
353.4'0973—dc21   2002014672

Table of Contents

The Government's Lawyer

More than 200 years ago, a group of men wrote a document, the U.S. Constitution, which established the American government. The authors of the Constitution divided the government into three separate branches. These branches are the legislative branch, the judicial branch, and the executive branch.

Under the Constitution, the legislative branch was made up of the Senate and the House of Representatives. The president led the executive branch. The judicial branch was the nation's court system, with the Supreme Court as the highest court.

The Supreme Court building in Washington, D.C., is home to the nation's highest court.

This building in Washington, D.C., houses the Department of Justice.

The people who enforce the nation's laws work in the Department of Justice. This department has six parts. Each one handles a different area of the law, such as business, civil rights, or crime. One person makes sure this huge legal operation runs smoothly. This person is the U.S. attorney general.

The attorney general's position was one of the first to be created by the government of the United States. In 1789, Congress passed the Judiciary Act, which set up the office of the attorney general. At that time, there was no Department of Justice.

Janet Reno was the first woman U.S. attorney general. She served under President Bill Clinton from 1993 to 2001.

Congress wanted the attorney general to be an expert in the law. He or she would serve as the government's legal adviser. It was not the attorney general's job to enforce the law. Instead, he or she would interpret it and represent the government in legal matters. For example, if someone sued the government, the attorney general would represent the United States in court. The attorney general also served as the prosecutor in cases that were argued before the Supreme Court.

As the United States grew larger in the years after 1789, legal problems became more common and more complicated. In 1829, President Andrew Jackson asked Congress to give the attorney general more power.

He especially wanted the attorney general to be in charge of collecting money that people and businesses owed to the government. Jackson also wanted the attorney general to supervise all trials that involved federal laws.

The presidents who came after Jackson wanted to give the attorney general more power, too. In 1845, President James K. Polk proposed the creation of a national law department. Congress was not sure that the attorney general should have more power, though. Its members would not take Polk's advice.

In 1870, Congress finally did set up the Department of Justice. The attorney general was the head of this new department. He or she was also a member of the cabinet—a group of advisers who help the president.

The attorney general is a member of the president's cabinet. Jeremiah Black (seated, right) served as attorney general from 1857 to 1860 under President James Buchanan (center).

The Attorney General's Responsibilities

The attorney general is the chief law officer of the government. One of the attorney general's main duties is to advise and represent the government in legal matters. When the president or Congress has a legal problem, such as a disagreement over whether a proposed action is against the law, the attorney general explains the law. He or she also describes what the government can or cannot do to fix the situation. The attorney general also suggests people for the president to appoint as federal judges or to serve in other legal positions.

On February 18, 1970, U.S. attorneys Dick Shultz (left) and Thomas Foran (right) held a press conference after an important trial. The attorney general oversees all U.S. attorneys.

The attorney general is in charge of U.S. marshals (pictured).

The attorney general is also in charge of the entire U.S. justice system. He or she oversees the work of the 93 U.S. attorneys, as well as all U.S. marshals, law clerks, and other federal court officers. U.S. attorneys work in all 50 states and in areas the United States controls, such as Puerto Rico, the Virgin Islands, Guam, and the Northern Marianas islands. These attorneys argue for the United States in criminal and civil lawsuits. The attorneys are the ones who actually take part in trials, but the attorney general supervises the cases. He or she is responsible for how the attorneys take care of these cases.

U.S. Attorney General John Ashcroft appeared before the Senate Judiciary Committee on December 6, 2001, to discuss national protection against terrorism.

National security is one of the attorney general's other areas of concern. He or she can interpret and even change the law to protect the United States from any sort of threat. After terrorists attacked the United States on September 11, 2001, for example, Attorney General John Ashcroft proposed many changes in the law. These changes would make it easier for the government to detain people who might be terrorists. They would also make it easier to gather evidence about people who work against the United States. Ashcroft and many other government leaders said these changes to the law were needed to prevent future attacks. Other people, though, worried that the attorney general's actions might take away the civil rights that the U.S. Constitution promises all Americans. Despite the debate, the changes were adopted. In cases like this one, the attorney general has to weigh the needs of the nation against the rights of individual citizens.

The Job of Attorney General

An attorney general spends much of his or her time in meetings. The attorney general has a great deal of contact with the president and members of Congress. As a member of the president's cabinet and the nation's top legal adviser, the attorney general meets often with the president to discuss important issues. The attorney general may also speak before Congress during legal investigations.

The attorney general also meets with different groups of people who support or oppose specific actions on legal matters, such as gun control. These meetings help the attorney general see how a law will affect the American people. They also show how laws can be put into effect in the best and easiest way.

Attorneys general often meet with other government leaders. This picture shows a 1938 meeting of Attorney General Homer Cummings (left) and J. Edgar Hoover, head of the FBI.

Janet Reno (center), like other attorneys general, made many public appearances, such as this news conference in 1998.

Legal cases and government hearings also take up a large part of the attorney general's day. He or she often speaks to committees that need legal information or want to know how the attorney general plans to deal with a certain issue.

The attorney general must also read thousands of pages of legal briefs and trial testimony. He or she does this to make sure U.S. attorneys do their jobs properly, and to stay informed about court decisions that affect how a law is enforced.

Attorney generals also make many public appearances. They speak to school and community groups, and at important government and business meetings. These appearances help teach the public about laws and how they are enforced and upheld.

Who Works with the Attorney General?

The attorney general has several attorneys to help him or her. The deputy attorney general works directly under the attorney general and is second in command in the department. The solicitor general is next in line. He or she represents the U.S. government in cases tried in the Supreme Court. The attorney general argued these cases in the early days of the nation's history, but he or she no longer does so today because of other official duties.

Deputy Attorney General Larry Thompson (center) served as second in command to Attorney General John Ashcroft.

Besides these two main assistants, the attorney general also has a large staff. The staff includes many law clerks. These people research earlier cases that involved the government. They collect information about these

The solicitor general represents the U.S. government in cases before the Supreme Court. Thurgood Marshall (right) was the first African American to hold the position of solicitor general.

cases and present what they find to the attorney general. With this information, the attorney general can see how laws have been understood and enforced in the past. This can show how a case might be argued in the future.

Lawyers who work for the attorney general often represent the United States in court. These lawyers gather evidence and interview witnesses to find information they can use in court to help the government win.

In addition to the legal team, a number of secretaries and other aides work for the attorney general. This support staff keeps records and handles the attorney general's correspondence. It also prepares a schedule of meetings, appearances, and other events that are part of the attorney general's day.

Where Does the Attorney General Work?

The attorney general's office is located in the Department of Justice building. This building is on Pennsylvania Avenue in Washington, D.C., near the White House. The Department of Justice building holds the offices of many law enforcement agencies. The attorney general also travels to other government locations, such as the White House, the Supreme Court building, and the headquarters of the Federal Bureau of Investigation (FBI).

Former U.S. attorney general Tom Clark posed for this picture in the attorney general's office, which is located in the Department of Justice building.

Who Can Become Attorney General?

Since the attorney general is the chief law officer of the government, he or she must have a strong legal background. In 1789, Congress said that the attorney general should be "a learned person in the law." Attorney generals have always been lawyers, and many have been judges. Several were state attorney generals before they became the U.S. attorney general. Others have worked as federal prosecutors.

> **USA FACT**
>
> Ten attorney generals have gone on to serve on the U.S. Supreme Court. Two of these, Roger B. Taney and Harlan F. Stone, became chief justices.

Harlan Stone became chief justice of the Supreme Court in 1941 after serving as attorney general under President Calvin Coolidge.

The Approval Process

Like other members of the cabinet, the attorney general is appointed by the president, but must be approved by the Senate. After the president names a candidate for attorney general, a Senate Judiciary Committee holds hearings to confirm or deny the appointment.

These Senate Judiciary Committee hearings can be difficult. There are 18 senators on the committee. Their job is to look into all aspects of the candidate's life and career.

Senate Judiciary Committee hearings are held to decide whether to approve the president's candidate for attorney general. This hearing was held in 2001 to evaluate the nomination of John Ashcroft by President George W. Bush.

This includes personal matters, such as family, as well as the person's conduct at work. The committee has the FBI do a criminal background check. Then, the

USA Fact

Attorney general candidates are not always confirmed by the Senate. In 1987, Robert Bork was not approved because his political opinions upset many people.

committee asks the candidate about his or her plans for the office. The senators may even ask the candidate for his or her opinion on certain issues. Each committee member has 30 minutes to ask questions. After all members have questioned the candidate, each one gets another 30 minutes to ask more questions.

The Senate Judiciary Committee reviews all aspects of a candidate's life. In 1993, Zoë Baird withdrew her nomination for attorney general after it was discovered that she had hired illegal immigrants to work in her home.

*After the attorney general is confirmed, he or she must be sworn in.
Edwin Meese was sworn in as attorney general in 1985.*

The hearings can last for just a few days, or as long as several weeks. At the end of the hearings, the committee votes to approve or reject the nomination. If the committee approves, the nomination goes to the full Senate for a vote. If a two-thirds majority of senators vote yes, the candidate is confirmed.

The new attorney general is usually sworn in within a day or two of his or her approval. He or she stands in front of the president, then puts one hand on a Bible and raises the other hand in the air. The new attorney general swears an oath to do the job faithfully and to obey the law.

A Time of Crisis

Over the years, attorney generals have faced many difficult moments. To enforce a law or deal with a legal challenge can sometimes be grueling.

The 1960s were a time of great social unrest. At that time, black people and white people were segregated, or kept apart, in almost every aspect of life. This was especially true in the southern states. Black students went to different schools that were not as good as white schools. Black citizens in the South had to sit in separate sections when they used public transportation. Some restaurants and hotels would not serve them.

Citizens in the South marched for equal civil rights for African Americans in the 1960s.

During the 1950s and 1960s, many Americans fought to win equal civil rights for African Americans. When Robert F. Kennedy was attorney general from 1961 to 1964, he made civil rights a priority. He worked hard to make sure civil rights laws were enforced. He also demanded that governors and other

In 1963, Attorney General Robert F. Kennedy (left) asked his brother, President John F. Kennedy (right), to protect civil rights activists by sending federal troops to protests and marches.

officials in the South protect those who fought for civil rights. When local officials did not keep civil rights activists safe, Kennedy encouraged his brother, President John F. Kennedy, to send federal troops to protect citizens and keep the peace. Robert Kennedy also spoke to members of the Interstate Commerce Commission (ICC), which regulated public transportation. He said that segregated buses, trains, and stations were against the law. In time, the ICC declared that all public transportation that went between the states had to give equal treatment to everyone, regardless of race.

Another Time of Crisis

Sometimes an attorney general's decision can have deadly results. On February 28, 1993, agents from the government's Bureau of Alcohol, Tobacco, and Firearms tried to arrest David Koresh. Koresh was a religious cult leader who lived with members of his group in Waco, Texas. The cult had a large number of illegal weapons. The attempt to arrest Koresh turned into a gun battle in which four agents were killed. For the next seven weeks, Koresh and many of his followers remained inside their compound.

On April 19, Attorney General Janet Reno allowed the FBI to break into the compound to arrest Koresh.

In 1993, David Koresh's compound burned down after FBI agents raided it. Attorney General Janet Reno had to appear before a House Judiciary Committee that investigated the disaster.

In 2000, U.S. attorney Mike Bradford (left) represented the United States against David Koresh's religious group, the Branch Davidians.

FBI agents charged into the compound with an armored vehicle. Then they pumped tear gas inside to try to force the cult members to come out. After the cult members shot at the agents, the compound exploded and burned to the ground. Koresh and 85 of his followers died.

Reno took full responsibility for the disaster. "I approved the plan and I'm responsible for it,"she said. She went on television and spoke to reporters. She explained why she had supported the raid and what she had hoped would happen. Reno also spoke to a House Judiciary Committee that looked into the tragedy. Six months later, the committee issued a report. It said that Reno had tried "all reasonable alternatives" before she had allowed the raid on Koresh's compound. The committee cleared her of any blame in the way the affair was handled.

The Attorney General's Day

The attorney general handles many different tasks during his or her workday. Here is what a typical day might be like:

6:30 AM   Wakes, showers, dresses, and has breakfast

8:00 AM   Arrives at the Department of Justice and looks over legal briefs and other paperwork

10:15 AM   Meets with the president and other cabinet members to discuss legal issues

11:00 AM   Attends a federal trial

1:00 PM   Eats lunch with members of legal staff

2:00 PM   Testifies before a congressional committee about the position of the United States on an international legal matter

4:00 PM   Meets with the president and cabinet members to discuss national security

5:00 PM   Returns to office to review paperwork and correspondence

6:30 PM   Returns home for a quick dinner

Attorneys general often make television appearances to discuss important issues. On September 10, 1970, Attorney General John N. Mitchell (left) appeared on the Dick Cavett (center) Show.

7:30 PM   Travels to a television studio to appear on a cable news program

8:30 PM   Appears on television to answer questions about legal issues and national security

10:30 PM   Returns home, reads the newspaper, and watches television

11:30 PM   Bed

Fascinating Facts

John J. Crittenden is the only attorney general who served three presidents: William Harrison, John Tyler, and Millard Fillmore. He later served as a member of the House of Representatives from 1861 to 1863.

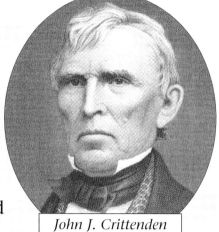

John J. Crittenden

Amos T. Akerman was the first attorney general to serve as head of the Department of Justice. He served under President Ulysses S. Grant from 1870 to 1871.

Amos T. Akerman

Alfonso Taft served as attorney general from 1876 to 1877. His son, William Howard Taft, was president from 1909 to 1913, and chief justice of the Supreme Court from 1921 to 1930.

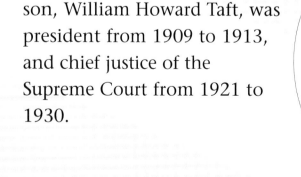

Alfonso Taft

William Pinckney, who served as attorney general from 1811 to 1814, argued many cases before the Supreme Court as a lawyer. But he never appeared before the Supreme Court in the role of attorney general.

William Pinckney

John F. Kennedy was the first president to nominate his brother—**Robert F. Kennedy**—to the position of attorney general

Robert F. Kennedy

Janet Reno

Janet Reno was the first woman to serve as attorney general. She served under President Bill Clinton from 1993 to 2001.

Ulysses S. Grant had five attorney generals—more than any other president.

Between 1870 and the end of the 19th century, the attorney general had to pay the Department of Justice's rent out of his own salary.

Early attorney generals worked part-time and often had their own private law practices at the same time that they served the government. This is no longer allowed.

Glossary

adviser—someone who works closely with a person in power and provides information and suggestions

cabinet—a group of advisers to the president, including federal department heads and the U.S. representative to the United Nations (UN)

civil—a type of legal case in which one citizen acts against another to recover money or rights

Constitution—the document that established the United States and includes the principles of the nation

criminal—a type of legal case that deals with a crime or illegal act

prosecutor—a lawyer who represents the government in a criminal trial

Griffin Bell (right) served as attorney general from 1977 to 1979 under President Jimmy Carter.

For More Information

Publications

Daniel E. Harmon. *The Attorney General's Office.* Philadelphia: Chelsea House Publishers, 2002.

Virginia Meachum. *Janet Reno: United States Attorney General.* Springfield, NJ: Enslow Publishers, Inc., 1995.

Robert F. Kennedy (center)

Robert H. Jackson (second from right) only served as attorney general from 1940 to 1941. In 1941, President Franklin D. Roosevelt nominated him to the Supreme Court.

Web Sites

Office of the Attorney General Home Page

http://www.usdoj.gov/ag/

This official Department of Justice site includes information about the attorney general's office, as well as links to transcripts of speeches and legal opinions given by the attorney general.

Index